Pooh

storybook
Treasury

MOUSE WORKS

Table of Contents

Stripes

The rain had just ended in the Hundred-Acre Wood and there were mud puddles everywhere.

We all know mud puddles were made for splashing in. And that's exactly what Tigger was doing.

"Hoo-Hoo-Hoooo," said Tigger, "there's a good one!" as he landed in a really big puddle.

Suddenly, Pooh, Piglet and Rabbit ran out from some nearby bushes. Pooh and Rabbit grabbed Tigger by the arms and legs. Piglet grabbed him by the tail.

Rabbit counted, "One, two, threeee!" as they hurled Tigger into the air.

Muddy Tigger landed in a great big wooden tub full of water and suds.

"If you're going to bounce in mud puddles, you're going to take baths!" said Rabbit as he ran to the tub of suds, followed by Pooh and Piglet.

And they all began scrubbing Tigger with scrub brushes.

When they were done scrubbing Tigger, Rabbit doused him with a bucket of water to rinse him off.

And when he stepped out of the tub, Tigger was
surprised to see that he had no stripes!

"Who are you?" asked Piglet.

"Tigger!" said Tigger. "Who else would I be, for goodness
sakes?"

"Why, you couldn't possibly be Tigger," said Rabbit.
"Tiggers have stripes!"

"He has two ears and a tail," said Piglet. "Maybe he's a rabbit!"

Tigger stretched his ears.

Then he tugged Rabbit's ears.

"Hey, yeah!" said Tigger. "And Rabbit doesn't have any stripes, either! Maybe I am a rabbit! Wait a minute! I don't know how to be a rabbit! What do I do?"

Rabbit escorted Tigger to his garden to give him his first lesson in being a rabbit.

"The most important thing to a rabbit is his garden," said Rabbit.

"And your first lesson in being a rabbit is to use this pest spray to protect my prize-winning tomatoes. Don't let any pests near them!" warned Rabbit.

"I'll guard your tomatoes as if they were my very own vegebubbles, fellow rabbit!" declared Tigger.

Rabbit left, and Tigger began marching back and forth, guarding the garden.

Suddenly he stopped marching. A noise coming from one of the tomato plants had caught his ear. "Halt! Who crawls there?" yelled Tigger.

It was a hungry little bug.

"Aww...you're hungry, huh, bugsy boy?"

The hungry little bug nodded 'yes.'

"Well, I guess one little tomato wouldn't hurt. Just don't tell the other rabbit, okay?"

And with that, Tigger plucked a nice, juicy tomato and gave it to the hungry little bug.

The bug ate the tomato with one bite!

Just then, Rabbit returned and saw what had happened.

"Oh, no!" he exclaimed. "You didn't! You did!"

"Aw, what's the big deal, fellow rabbit?" said Tigger. "It's just one hungry, defenseless little bug."

"But, you don't understand," said Rabbit. "He'll tell his friends where there's food, and…"

TOMATOES

But it was too late. Rabbit's garden was gone. He and Tigger stood in the middle of a devastated tomato field. There were remnants of tomatoes dripping off the vines and countless bloated, contented, fat little bugs lying around, digesting.

"Get out!" screamed Rabbit as he chased Tigger out of what used to be his garden. "Get out of here, you pest!"

Tigger ran as fast as he could, with Rabbit right behind him, spraying furiously.

Tigger found a nice tree to lean on as he settled down to catch his breath. Just then he saw Winnie the Pooh chasing a butterfly through the trees.

"Sayyy…I wonder," wondered Tigger, "if I'm a bear!"

Pooh gave Tigger his first lesson in being a bear.

He showed him how to climb a honey tree and get honey out of a beehive.

But Tigger accidentally knocked the hive out of the tree and all the angry bees chased him deep into the woods.

Pooh found Tigger sitting dejectedly under a tree.
"I don't think I want to be a bear," said Tigger. "Maybe
I'm a piglet."
So, Pooh and Tigger went to Piglet's house to find out.

After they got there, Tigger tried on some of Piglet's shirts. They were much too small for him. One of Piglet's shirts just barely fit onto one of Tigger's legs.

"I'm afraid you're too big to be a piglet," said Piglet. "We can't all be small animals."

"But the stripes look good on you," said Pooh.

"Heyyy! Maybe I'm a tigger!" declared Tigger.

"No, I'm afraid there's only one," said Pooh, "and he has stripes."

"Maybe we could paint stripes on him," said Piglet.

So Pooh and Piglet painted stripes on Tigger, and when they were done, Tigger was so happy he started bouncing with joy.

"I'm a tigger! I'm a tigger."

He was so happy to have stripes that he bounced right out the door.

Suddenly, there was a loud clap of thunder, and it began to rain.

Tigger's new stripes ran down his body and onto the ground in puddles. Dejected and dripping, Tigger shook his head slowly.

"I'm not a tigger!"

In the moonlight the rain dripped to a stop.
"I'm not a tigger...I'm not a rabbit...I'm not a
bear...and I'm sure not a piglet," he sniffed.
"I'm not an anything."

Just then Eeyore walked by.

"Hello, Tigger," said Eeyore.

"Hello, Eeyore," answered Tigger.

"Hey! You called me Tigger!"

"Well, aren't you?" asked Eeyore.

"No," said Tigger, "I don't have any stripes!"

"Aw, it doesn't matter. You're still a tigger on the inside. You'll always be Tigger," said Eeyore.

"Yeahhh-hoooo!!" screamed Tigger, jumping wildly in the air.

Tigger bounced happily around Eeyore, using his tail like a giant spring.

Suddenly, Tigger's tail went out of control, and he landed hard on his bottom.

With a loud "POP!" a stripe popped onto Tigger's tail.
"Yahoo!" yelled Tigger, as he started to bounce even
more.

And as he did so, more and more stripes popped on all
over his body.

Winnie the Pooh, Piglet and Rabbit came out to see what all the noise was about. Tigger came bouncing past them like a Tigger with a mission.

"Now I'm Tigger on the outside and Tigger on the inside, too!"

And as he bounced off into the sunset, he shouted, "And I've got a lot of bouncing to catch up on!"

Paw and Order

Kanga and Roo sat in front of a stage in the Hundred-Acre Wood. A play called *Paw and Order* was about to begin.

As the curtains opened, Gopher and Owl sang about the play's hero:

"This hero made an outlaw tame,
And Sheriff Piglet is his name!"

The curtains opened all the way, and Owl and Gopher left the stage. Kanga and Roo could see a blistering-hot desert. A party of hardy pioneers rolled across the dry wasteland in a stagecoach.

"Water! Water!" choked Tigger.

"Honey! Honey!" gasped Winnie the Pooh.

At last the pioneers came to Rickety Gulch, a little prairie town. They stopped in front of the saloon. All the townsfolk ran out to warn them.

"Run for your lives!" they yelled. "A gang of horse thieves is comin' to town! We're clearin' out!"

"Oh! Perhaps we should tell the sheriff," suggested Piglet.

"Sheriff!" shouted one of the townsfolk. "We have no sheriff. But *you* can be sheriff!" he said, pinning a badge on Piglet.

"M - m - m - me!" stammered Piglet, shaking nervously.

Just then, a cloud of dust and the thunder of hooves rumbled up Main Street.

"It's the horse thieves!" cried the townsfolk.

Winnie the Pooh and his pals found themselves surrounded by Nasty Jack and his nasty gang.

"I see you have a badge on," snorted Nasty Jack to Piglet. "You must be the sheriff. Me and sheriffs don't get along."

Then Nasty Jack and his gang put Pooh, Piglet, Tigger and Rabbit back in their stagecoach and shoved it down the hill. Pooh and his pals crashed right into the sheriff's office.

As they picked themselves up, they tried to decide what to do.

"I'm getting out of here," said Rabbit, and he ran down the street. But as he passed by the saloon's swinging doors, Nasty Jack grabbed him.

"Howdy, Buckaroo," said Nasty Jack. "You the proprietor of this establishment?"

"N - n - n - no!" stammered Rabbit.

"Then you must be a friend of the sheriff," said Nasty Jack, "and since I hate sheriffs…"

Rabbit knew that if he admitted he was a friend of the sheriff, he'd be in trouble. So he quickly zipped behind the bar to take their orders.

"Banana splits all around!" ordered Nasty Jack. "And pronto!"

As fast as he could, Rabbit made banana splits and served them to Nasty Jack and his gang.

When Nasty Jack got his banana split, he asked, "What?
No cherry?"

Nasty Jack grabbed Rabbit by the neck.

"Let me answer that," coughed Rabbit, "by
saying…HELLLLP!"

Pooh, Piglet, Tigger and Eeyore had followed Rabbit and saw what was happening.

"Rabbit's in trouble!" gasped Pooh.

"What should we do, Pooh?" asked Piglet.

"You're the sheriff, Piglet," answered Pooh. "You have to give *us* orders."

"Well, then," said Piglet, "I order you to think of something!"

"I've got it!" said Tigger, bouncing with joy. "I'll go in the front door an' keep 'em occupied, while Pooh and Eeyore go in the back door an' rescue ol' long ears!"

"What'll *I* do?" asked Piglet.

"You stay here, lookin' sheriffy," said Tigger, "and when we're all set, you give the signal to *go!*"

When everybody was ready, Piglet gave the signal.
"R-r-ready? G-g-go!" shouted Piglet.
Tigger bounced boldly into the saloon.

"Ki-yi whoopeeyay!" sang Tigger. "I'm gonna rope ya, sonny, if ya don't drop that bunny!"

Nasty Jack dropped Rabbit, and watched in disbelief as Tigger twirled his lariat and did all sorts of rope tricks.

Meanwhile, Pooh and Eeyore sneaked in the back door.

But Nasty Jack's gang was ready for them. As soon as Pooh and Eeyore entered the room, some of the horse thieves dropped barrels over them and rolled them right back out into the street.

Other horse thieves tied up Tigger and Rabbit while Nasty Jack grabbed Piglet and plunked him down on the bar.

"Well, sheriff," sneered Nasty Jack, "it looks like it's trouncin' time for you and your pals."

Suddenly, the swinging doors flew open, and in stomped THE MASKED BEAR, accompanied by his faithful steed.

"Freeze!" said the Masked Bear. "If you please."

With his spurs "ching-ching-chinging" across the floor, the Masked Bear faced Nasty Jack.

"And who are you?" asked Nasty Jack.

"I am the Masked Bear," said the Masked Bear, "and this is my faithful steed."

Slowly, Nasty Jack reached behind the bar and pulled out a huge scoop of strawberry ice cream. Without warning, he flipped the ice cream at the Masked Bear.

The Masked Bear ducked out of the way of the flying ice cream, tripped over his faithful steed, rolled across the floor and crashed into the player piano.

The music roll popped out of the piano, rolled across the floor and hit Nasty Jack in the ankles.

Nasty Jack fell to the floor and rolled right out the door.
He landed in the watering trough in front of the saloon.
With a splash, a sputter and a spurt, Nasty Jack shook the
water out of his face.

While everyone was busy laughing, Piglet was busy
cutting the ropes on Rabbit and Tigger. They all escaped
back to the sheriff's office.

Nasty Jack and his gang stuffed the Masked Bear and
his faithful steed back into barrels and rolled them out the
door.

The Masked Bear and his faithful steed rolled down the
hill, all the way to the edge of Rickety Gulch Canyon.

Soon, a telegram came for Sheriff Piglet. "Dear Sheriff," it read, "be on the streets at sundown. (signed) Nasty Jack."

"I just remembered," said Piglet, "I have a very important appointment…heh-heh-heh…under my bed!"

"But, Piglet," said Tigger, "you *have* to face Nasty Jack! All the townsfolk are depending on you."

Just then, all the townsfolk, who had been hiding under the floorboards and in the cracks in walls, popped out and cheered, "Yeah!"

"B - b - b - but…well…oh, okay," said Piglet.

As the late afternoon sun settled on the horizon, the main street was dusty and deserted. Silhouetted against the fading light of day, Nasty Jack stood in the middle of the street, waiting for Sheriff Piglet. Nervously, Piglet stepped into the street to face him.

Piglet was so nervous, every inch of his little body shook like a leaf.

"M - m - Mr. Nasty Jack, sir," sputtered poor Piglet, "as sh - sh - sheriff of this town, I p - p - p - place you under arrest, if you don't mind."

At that moment, because he was shaking so much, Piglet's badge popped off!

"Now look what you did!" snarled Nasty Jack. "Your badge fell off! You know what that means?"

"I'm n - not sheriff anymore?" asked Piglet.

"You're not sheriff anymore!" snorted Nasty Jack. "That's just peachy! Now who am I going to trounce? What am I going to do?"

"Ahh…maybe *you* could be sheriff," suggested Piglet.

"Honest?" asked Nasty Jack, a smile creeping across his face. "Ya mean it? I always *wanted* to be a sheriff!"

Nasty Jack proudly put on the sheriff's badge and turned to his gang of horse thieves. "All right, pilgrims! *I'm* the sheriff now…and I'm *really* gonna clean up this town!" he snarled at them. "UNDERSTAND?"

And with that, all of Nasty Jack's gang high-hoofed it out of town. All the townsfolk cheered as they came out of their hiding places. At last, peace came to Rickety Gulch.

As the sun set on the western horizon, Pooh and Eeyore
finally got out of the barrels at the edge of Rickety Gulch
Canyon.

"I'm thirsty," said Pooh. "Let's go get a sarsaparilla."

"Lead the way," said Eeyore.

When they got back to the saloon, everyone joined them
in a root-beer toast to the new sheriff of Rickety Gulch.

Christopher Robin began to close the curtains.

After the curtains drew shut, Kanga and Roo applauded. Pooh, Piglet, Tigger, Eeyore and Rabbit came through the curtains to take a bow. Owl and Gopher returned to the stage to sing:

"And so the legend has been told
Of Sheriff Piglet, brave and bold.
A hero and a loyal friend,
He gives this tale a happy end."

Eeyore's Tail Tale

Eeyore sighed, watching Rabbit hop around his garden. Rabbit was chasing bugs, but Eeyore thought he was dancing.

"Wish I could dance," said Eeyore.

Eeyore tried to copy Rabbit's dance step, but he stepped on his tail and fell.

"Not again!" Eeyore said, annoyed. That tail of his was forever coming off, and he was pretty tired of it.

He rose and walked away, leaving his tail in the mud.

Rabbit charged into his carrot patch. "All right, you pests," he said, grabbing his bug sprayer. "You asked for it!"

He sprayed until there was a billowing cloud covering his garden. When it cleared, the garden seemed to be deserted.

"Where'd those little bugbarians go?" asked Rabbit. Suddenly, the bugs appeared behind him with a big board.

Thwack! The bugs knocked Rabbit over the fence. He landed in the mud next to Eeyore's tail.

"*Ick!*" said Rabbit, wiping the mud off his face. When he sat up, he saw an army of bugs marching towards him, aiming the bug spray in his direction.

"Oh, dearie dear!"

Rabbit frantically searched for something he could use to defend himself. When he spotted Eeyore's tail, he snatched it up.

"Don't come any closer!" warned Rabbit, swinging the tail. "I've got. . . er. . . THIS!"

To Rabbit's surprise, the bugs came to a complete halt. The leader's eyes nearly popped out, and his heart beat wildly. He howled and whistled, and started trembling all over. Then, before Rabbit could blink, the leader of the bugs ran up to Eeyore's tail and hugged it to his tiny body. Obviously, it was love at first sight. But what could a bug see in Eeyore's tail?

"Hmm!" said Rabbit thoughtfully. "This gives me an idea." And he took the tail off to his house.

By now, Eeyore was beginning to miss his tail. For one thing, he was a lot colder back there.

Suddenly Tigger bounced up and knocked Eeyore flat. "Hoo-hoo-HOO! Hiya, Donkey Boy! Say, I almost didn't recollect you without your tail."

"We parted company at Rabbit's," explained Eeyore. "I'm much happier without it. Can't you tell?"

Tigger studied Eeyore's face, which looked as gloomy as ever.

"How'll you be able to tell your front from your back without a tail?" asked Tigger. "And since you're always sayin' you're such a nobody, won't you be even less of a somebody with part of you missin'?"

The corners of Eeyore's mouth drooped a little lower.

"You're right. But, how can I get the little guy back?"

"Hoo-hoo! Have no fear — Private Ear Tigger is here! And reunitin' loved ones is what Private Ears do best!"

Back at Rabbit's house, Eeyore's tail had taken on a new look. Using bits of paper and some glue, Rabbit turned Eeyore's tail into a lady caterpillar.

"Now that's what I call a Worm Wrangler!" said Rabbit, sticking Eeyore's tail on the end of a fishing pole. Then Rabbit dangled the tail in front of the bugs and led them to a stream.

"Good-bye! Have a wonderful trip!" called Rabbit, waving to them as they sailed downstream in a shoebox.

Later, Winnie the Pooh knocked on Rabbit's door.

"Hello, Pooh," said Rabbit. "How are you this great day?"

Pooh saw the tail dangling from Rabbit's fishing rod. "What's that?" asked Pooh.

"This? Oh, nothing," said Rabbit, as he quickly hid the fishing rod behind his back. Rabbit didn't realize that Eeyore's tail had dropped off. "Now, excuse me, Pooh," said Rabbit. He slipped into the house and slammed the door.

Pooh picked Eeyore's tail up off the ground.

"If this thing means nothing to Rabbit," said Pooh, "I think I'll find a use for it."

Meanwhile, Tigger was still trying to help Eeyore find his tail. He was certain that someone had stolen it, but who? Rabbit lived close by, so Tigger decided to question him first.

Moments later, Rabbit threw open the door, and in bounced Tigger.

"Gotcha!" said Tigger, knocking Rabbit flat.

"What?"

"Where were you the night o' the forty-third?" demanded Private Ear Tigger. "When was the next-to-the-last time you saw Eeyore's tail?"

"Eeyore's tail?" repeated Rabbit. "What do you mean?"

As Tigger was explaining, Rabbit noticed that his Worm Wrangler was missing. It was another case for the Private Ear!

"But what about my tail?" asked Eeyore.

"Not now, Eeyore," said Rabbit and Tigger.

"Who was the last no-good-nik you saw?" asked Tigger.

"Why, it was Pooh Bear," asked Rabbit. "But he's. . ."

"A case of Very Little Brain goin' bad!" declared Tigger.

Eeyore sighed. Wasn't anyone going to find his tail?

Winnie the Pooh was sitting on a branch by a beehive, about to fill his honey pot.

"My tummy tells me this is a Bee Tickler!" said Pooh, looking at Eeyore's tail. He stuck the tail into the hive and wiggled it around. Several bees fell out, laughing.

"I was right!" said Pooh, reaching inside. He crammed some honey into his mouth. The bees glared at him.

"Uh-oh!" said Pooh, gulping. "Tickle, tickle?"

The angry bees swooped down on Pooh and tumbled him and his honey pot off the limb. Eeyore's tail landed on a thorny bush.

"Oh, bother!" said Pooh as he fell. When he hit the ground, the honey pot got jammed on his head.

"Is it time for a midnight smackerel already?" asked Pooh. He couldn't see a thing. Then he tripped and tumbled down the hill.

Pooh barreled into Tigger, Rabbit and Eeyore. When they rolled to a stop, Rabbit yanked Pooh's honey pot off his head.

"Tryin' to disguise yourself, Buddy Bear?" said Tigger.

"Where's my Worm Wrangler?" demanded Rabbit.

"What about my tail?" asked Eeyore.

"Not now, Eeyore!" said Rabbit and Tigger.

But Pooh knew nothing about a tail, or a Worm Wrangler. "I'm missing my Bee Tickler," said Pooh. "Perhaps Mr. Private Ear can help me find it."

"I love this job!" said Tigger, bouncing.

"Forward, men!" said Tigger. He peered under every rock and around every tree in the Hundred-Acre Wood. But he walked right past the bush where Eeyore's tail was hanging.

Piglet saw his friends hurry by and wondered where everyone was going.

"Oh, my!" thought Piglet. "Perhaps they're looking for s-something scary!"

Piglet suddenly spotted Eeyore's tail.

"Oh, d-dear! That certainly looks like a very small part of a Very Large Animal," said Piglet. Since Piglet was a Very Small Animal himself, he trembled fearfully and backed away. He backed into a branch behind him. Startled, he jumped up into the air and landed right by Eeyore's tail.

When Piglet saw that nothing was attached to the tail, he was relieved. He picked it up. "You might come in handy for protecting me from spookables!" he said.

When he reached home, Piglet made himself a Bully Bamboozler — a small Heffalump made from a balloon, with Eeyore's tail for a trunk.

Meanwhile, not far away, Tigger was thinking hard.

"Who would want Eeyore's tail? It has to be one pitiful little termite!" said Tigger.

"Piglet's little and pitiful," suggested Eeyore.

"Piglet! That's it!" said Tigger. He drew a "Wanted" poster that was supposed to look like Piglet, although it didn't. Then he bounced off to Piglet's house.

"Look!" said Pooh, pointing straight at Piglet's Bully Bamboozler. It looked like the fellow in Tigger's poster.

"Grab him!" yelled Tigger, pouncing on the balloon. There was a loud pop, and Eeyore's tail went flying.

Owl flew by at that very moment.

"My word!" said Owl, swooping down to grab Eeyore's tail. "This looks like my Uncle Torbett's bell rope!" And off Owl flew with his new prize.

Tigger looked up as Owl flew by with Eeyore's tail.

"It's time we get to the top of this mess!" said Tigger.

But all Eeyore cared about was his tail.

Tigger bounced up to Owl's house and pulled the bell rope right off the door. "They don't make them like they used to," said Tigger.

When Owl came to the door, Tigger bounced in and threw the bell rope down on a chair accusing Owl of taking it. Eeyore backed into the chair and sat down sharply on the bell rope. When it stuck him, he jumped into the center of the room. His friends stared.

"My Worm Wrangler!"

"My Bee Tickler!"

"My B-Bully B-Bamboozler!"

"Uncle Torbett's Bell Rope!"

Tigger yanked off Eeyore's tail and held it up as evidence.

"I know no one cares except me," said Eeyore sadly, "but that's my tail!"

"Wait, Eeyore! That's it!" said Tigger. "Your tail plotted its own disappearance so you would learn to appreciate it! I knew it all along!"

Tigger pinned the tail back onto the smiling Eeyore.

"Well, from now on," said Eeyore, "my tail and I are going to stick together — no matter what!"

Pooh

Rabbit Marks the Spot

One day, Winnie the Pooh, Piglet, Tigger and Gopher dressed up like pirates to dig for treasure in Rabbit's garden. When Rabbit saw them digging up his precious vegetables, he was ready to blow his top.

"What is going on here?" demanded Rabbit.

"It's us, Rabbit!" said Pooh, thinking Rabbit didn't recognize them. After all, they were all dressed like pirates.

"We're digging for treasure," explained Gopher.

"Not in *my* garden!" yelled Rabbit.

"Oh, d-dear!" said Piglet, panicking.

KERIiTS

CABEGE

PUNKINS

Piglet and his gang of pirates ran to their land-ship and shoved off.

"Poop the sail deck!" yelled Captain Piglet. "Swab the mizzenmast! Foot the yardarm!"

Unfortunately, a strong wind blew the land-ship back into the garden. It plowed up all the vegetables, and flattened Rabbit, too.

"I'm not going to get mad," said Rabbit with clenched teeth. "I'm going to teach them a lesson!"

PEES

Later that day, in a remote spot somewhere in the Hundred-Acre Wood, Rabbit put the finishing touches on his plan.

"So, Captain Piglet and his pitiful pirates want to find buried treasure, do they?" said Rabbit, shoving a rock-filled chest into a hole. "I'll give them a treasure. . . a worthless one!"

Rabbit filled the hole with dirt, then grabbed a piece of paper and scrawled something on it.

"I'll give them a map to help them find it!" he said, grinning. Then he stuffed the map into a bottle, took the bottle to the river, and threw it in.

Not much later, the runaway land-ship crashed on the bank of the river. Pooh looked up and saw a bottle floating toward them. When he waded out to get the bottle, he found that it had Rabbit's map inside. He showed the others.

"Bunny Boy, look what we found!" said Tigger when Rabbit walked up.

"A real treasure map!" said Gopher.

"Why, so you have!" said Rabbit, acting surprised. "This map belonged to my great-great-great uncle Long John Cottontail, a famous pirate!"

"Don't worry, Rabbit," said Tigger. "Findin' treasure's what Captain Piglet and his pirates do best! Hoo-hoo-hoo!"

Piglet studied the map, then set out to find the treasure.
Pooh and the others joined the search, while Rabbit watched
from a distance, laughing.

"Now, let's see," said Piglet. "Twelve paces from the
river. . . then turn right, twenty-two steps to the old hollow
log. . . ten paces from the rock, then —"

"Wait a minute!" said Tigger, cutting Piglet off. "Long
John Cottontail didn't mean those little piglety paces. He
meant big piratey steps!" Tigger took the map from Piglet.
"Let's see, six paces to the tree. . ."

Tigger's paces led straight into Rabbit's front room. He and the others pulled out their shovels and started digging.

"Hiya, Rabbit!" called Tigger when Rabbit appeared at the front door.

Rabbit sputtered, waving his arms wildly as he looked at the huge hole in the middle of his room. He was so furious, he couldn't speak.

"Don't worry, Fluffy-Face," said Tigger, thinking Rabbit was worried about being left out. "When we find the treasure, we'll split it with ya!"

"Aaaarrrrrrgh!" screamed Rabbit.

Rabbit grabbed the map and led the group back into the woods.

"Don't you pirates know how to read a map?" asked Rabbit. He came to a stop and pointed to a large X painted in the dirt. "*There's* the X that marks the spot!" said Rabbit.

Tigger, excited, hugged everyone. "The treasure! We found it, and it's exakakly what I always dreamed of! My very own big 'X'!"

Rabbit sighed impatiently. "The treasure's *under* the 'X', Tigger."

"Oh," said Tigger.

Pooh, Piglet, Gopher and Tigger dug until they hit something solid.

"We found it!" cried Piglet, brushing the dirt off the treasure chest.

"Well, what are we waiting for?" asked Gopher. "Let's get it open!"

"W-wait!" said Piglet. "Maybe we should take it to a safe place first."

Tigger agreed. "We better stash it somewhere else," he suggested.

"Somewhere secure," offered Pooh.

"Sssomewhere sssecret, sssonny!" added Gopher.

Pooh and the gang carried the chest to Piglet's house. Once the place was protected, they set the chest down and tried to pry it open with a pole.

"I can't wait!" said Pooh. "What do you suppose is inside?"

"Probably a whole bunch of fun stuff," replied Tigger.

"But then again," said Pooh, hopefully, "it could be honey."

"Honey, Pooh?" said Piglet, bending the pole as far back as it would go.

"Well," said Pooh, grabbing the pole to help Piglet. "I'd fill a treasure chest with honey!"

Suddenly, the pole snapped back, flipping Pooh and Piglet up in the air.

Pooh and Piglet fell back to the ground. As they dusted themselves off from their fall, Tigger and Gopher thought of another way to get the chest open.

The two disappeared into the woods and returned lugging a giant log. Then, on the count of three, they charged at the chest. Unfortunately, they completely missed it, and crashed into Piglet's front door, instead.

"Oh, d-dear!" cried Piglet.

Next, they tried to break the chest open by dropping it from the ceiling. But when they let the chest go, it crashed straight through the floor.

"Where'd it go?" asked Piglet.

"To the basement," answered Tigger.

"But I don't have a basement," said Piglet.

Tigger grinned sheepishly. "You do now!" he said.

"I've got it!" said Gopher. "Tomorrow, when it's light enough for us to see what we're doing, we'll blast the thing open with dynamite!"

Rabbit had watched all that went on through Piglet's window, and he couldn't have been more pleased with himself.

"I never dreamed the trick would turn out so well!" Rabbit said to himself when he got home. "When they find that chest is full of rocks, they'll think twice about tearing up gardens!"

Rabbit pulled back the covers on his bed. "Ah, Rabbit, you are a genius! An absolute genius!" he yawned, lying down for a nap.

Still wearing a smile on his face, Rabbit drifted off to sleep, and soon found himself in the middle of a strange dream.

Rabbit dreamed he was surrounded by giant talking rocks shaped a lot like Pooh, Piglet, Tigger and Gopher. The rocks seemed to glare at him.

"It wasn't very n-nice giving us a fake t-treasure," said Piglet Rock.

"You built up all our hopes," accused Pooh Rock.

"You got us all exciterated!" exploded Tigger Rock.

"And what'd we get? A bunch of rocks!" shouted Gopher Rock.

Frightened, Rabbit went down on his knees, begging for mercy. "I-I'm sorry! It was a joke!" explained Rabbit. "It was just a joke!"

"It was a joke, just a joke!" Rabbit muttered in his sleep. Then his eyes popped open, and he sat bolt upright in bed.

"Oh!" said Rabbit, looking around the room. "It was just a bad dream!"

Rabbit got out of bed and began to pace the floor with his head in his hands.

"Oh, what have I done?" he groaned. "When they find out what's in that chest, they'll hate me forever! Unless," said Rabbit, suddenly hopeful, "unless I get it back before they open it! But how?"

Rabbit thought for a long time before he came up with an idea.

Later that day, Piglet panicked when he looked out the window and saw the ghost of Long John Cottontail. Actually, it was Rabbit dressed up to look like his great-great-great uncle.

"Harrrr!" growled Rabbit, "I've come for what's mine!"

"Er, you better go talk to him, Captain Piglet!" said Tigger, frightened.

"P-perhaps we sh-should just give him his treasure," suggested Piglet.

Gopher didn't want to give up the chest, and neither did Pooh. Instead, they lowered the drawbridge on Rabbit's head, flattening him.

"Goodness!" said Pooh, peering out. "He seems to have disappeared!"

"Well, let's open the chest before that ghostie comes back!" said Tigger.

Defeated, Rabbit dragged himself to the window and looked in.

"Don't forget," said Piglet. "We must share the treasure with Rabbit."

"Share. . . with me?" thought Rabbit, listening.

"If Rabbit hadn't shown us where to d-dig, we never would've found the t-treasure," said Captain Piglet. "Part of it is his."

Rabbit shook his head sadly, turning away. "When they see those rocks, they'll never speak to me again!" thought Rabbit. "The only thing left for me to do is move away."

The next morning, Rabbit hurriedly packed up his belongings. He was tossing everything onto a wagon when Pooh and Tigger walked up.

"Rabbit! Rabbit!" called Pooh and Tigger. Neither of them seemed to notice the wagon overflowing with Rabbit's belongings. "We're going to open the treasure," said Pooh, grabbing Rabbit by the arm. "Come on!"

"No! No! I don't want any part of it!" protested Rabbit.

"He doesn't want any part of it! What an unselfish guy!" said Tigger.

Pooh and Tigger dragged Rabbit near Pooh's house. Rabbit's eyes widened when he saw the chest surrounded by bundles of dynamite. Gopher was wiring the dynamite to set off the explosion, and Piglet watched.

"No, no, please, no!" cried Rabbit.

"Aww, don't worry," said Gopher. "One push of this dingie and the whole thing goes kabingie! Ten, nine, eight, blassst off!"

Gopher pushed the plunger.

"NOOOO!" shouted Rabbit.

Finally, the chest was open. Rabbit tried to cover it with his body. "No! Don't look!" said Rabbit, thinking quickly. "Uncle Long John's such a kidder! Probably put the treasure in some other chest!"

Looking at Rabbit strangely, Tigger started to pry Rabbit's arms off the chest. Rabbit grabbed for the chest again, with a desperate look on his face.

"No! He. . . he. . . he forgot to put a treasure in it!" said Rabbit, talking very fast. "Uncle Long John — so absent-minded — buried an empty chest!"

"Oh, all right!" cried Rabbit. "I confess! It was me! I put the rocks in there!" Rabbit waited for his friends to yell at him, but they said nothing. "There never was a treasure!" said Rabbit. "I'm sorry. I'm sorry!"

Piglet and the others were confused. Ignoring Rabbit, they inched up to the chest and looked inside.

"This will keep my chair from wobbling!" said Pooh, grabbing a rock.

"Jussst what I need to prop up my winchbolts!" declared Gopher.

"Fantastical!" breathed Tigger. "What a great nutcracker!"

"It's every treasure we ever dreamed of!" said Piglet.

Rabbit pointed to the rocks in disbelief. "But, they're only. . ."

"And this is your share, Bunny Boy," said Tigger, handing one of the rocks to Rabbit.

"But, uh. . . but. . ."

"It's all right," said Piglet. "You take it — though it *is* a rare and valuable doorstop..."

"Probably belonged to your Uncle Long John!" guessed Tigger.

Rabbit was touched. "Why, I hardly know what to say," began Rabbit.

"But we do," said Piglet. "Thank you for helping us find this treasure."

"And thank you for this rare and valuable, uh, doorstop," said Rabbit.

While the group stood around the treasure chest, admiring their rocks, a ghost appeared from out of nowhere.

"A-har! Ya found me buried rocks, didya?" said Long John.

"Ghoooooost!" yelled Rabbit, Tigger, Piglet and Pooh and Gopher. And they all ran for their lives.